THE *T*OWER
AT THE *E*DGE
OF THE
*W*ORLD

THE TOWER
AT THE EDGE
OF THE
WORLD

VICTORIA GODDARD

Underhill
Books

Grandview, PEI, 2016

First published in electronic form in 2015.
First print edition published in 2016 by Underhill Books.

This is a work of fiction.
All of the characters portrayed in this story are either products of the author's imagination or are used fictitiously.

ISBN: 978-09937522-61

Underhill Books
4183 Murray Harbour Drive
RR#3 Belfast PEI
C0A 1A0 Canada
www.underhillbooks.com

THE TOWER
AT THE EDGE
OF THE
WORLD

I

In a tower at the edge of the world a young man found, one day, three items of interest: a golden key, an aphorism, and a spell.

He wasn't looking for them. He'd been living in the tower for a while by that point, and had settled into the rituals and routines of what he assumed would be the rest of a long and very quiet life. The intervals between rituals were taken up with playing the harp, reading poetry, or studying the most abstruse realms of theoretical magic.

The situation of the tower was at the easternmost edge of a long narrow island that broke the water's plummet into the Abyss on the eastern side of the world.

(He was not certain which world it was, but guessed

from the island and the sea that it was Colhélhé, though it might also have been some far reach of Voonra or Ysthar or even Alinor; he knew from the books in the tower and the magic that he was still within the bounds of the Empire, but only barely.) From the upper windows he could see long low grassy dunes, extending north and south until they dissolved into the blue distance.

Westward lay the rest of the world, and the Empire of Astandalas of which he was perhaps both loneliest outpost and most loyal son, and what he thought of as the peopled lands. All he could see of them was the short sides of the long dunes and, in the middle distance, the long silver line of the sea.

East of the tower was the Abyss.

During the day grey and white clouds boiled ceaselessly there, broken only by the bravest and most audacious kingfishers and gulls seeking only they knew what treasures under the mist and the spray and the spume.

During the night the stars went all the way down, and nothing stirred but their slow wheeling progress across three-quarters of the celestial globe.

It was after his morning bath and before breakfast that the young man had paused to look out the window. From the bathing room he could see the swallows who nested on the eaves of the tower's windows and in a row along the waterspout gargoyles. While he was looking out at the swallows, he happened to follow one's flight down with his gaze, and saw a glint of gold on the gargoyle's neck.

Despite a lifetime of discouragement, he was a curious young man. He was entirely unaccustomed to physical exertion, however, and at first he couldn't think how he might possibly get at the gold thing to see what it was.

The gold thing glinted, though that side of the tower was in shadow, for it was located to the east of the Sun.

(One morning he had awoken to see that the mists had not risen, and the Sun come running in the shape of a giant tossing a fiery sphere before he let out a wild holler and leaped into the sky to run his course. The young man was very surprised but not quite shocked to see this, for he had very little experience of the peopled lands and had spent much time reading ancient epics about the Sun and the Moon and the youth of the nine worlds, and for all he knew that sort of thing happened all the time. He was somewhat disappointed that it had, however, only happened to him the once.)

The gold thing was peeking out of a pile of sticks placed between the ears of the gargoyle. The swallows made clay nests, so it had to be something else, a gull or a kingfisher or an albatross or some other bird for which he had no name.

The tower had several layers of crenellations. The gargoyle stuck some eight feet out over the Abyss from a cornice located perhaps five feet below the window. The young man looked, considered the endless boiling cloud directly below the gargoyle, considered also the fact that he was not supposed to leave the tower, and somewhat wistfully went on with his day.

★★★

Life in the Empire, or at least life as he knew it, was entirely governed by an elaborate series of deliberately incomprehensible actions, prayers, sacrifices, songs, and commandments intended to bind its citizens and the several worlds they inhabited into a complex web of magic, custom, habit, and obedience. The Schooled magic of the Empire was the most complete and successful system of governance there had ever been. On Ysthar and parts of Zunidh the Schooled wizards managed even the weather according to their principles.

The young man had been very carefully brought up. He believed that if he did not fulfil his ritual duties, the Empire would fall.

And so he anointed himself with the unguent provided in the day's flask and prayed for the long life and reign of the Emperor Eritanyr, Sun of his people, god of the friendless, prosperity of the faithful, prince of a hundred lands.

He felt guilty that his thoughts wandered often to that little golden glint in the bird's nest.

★★★

The enchanted pantry that provided his meals did not require any choice or preparation from him with respect to the symbolism of tableware or foodstuffs. He accepted the goblets of one or other colour of glass or metal, the plates or bowls or platters of wood or lacquer, white porcelain or celadon, the utensils of gold or silver or iron or bamboo or glass. He performed his prayers and he ate the food presented at the prescribed hours, and if he was curious on occasion about what he was eating and where it might have come from, well, he knew better than to dwell on those questions, when he so thoroughly knew the answer to the question of *why*.

Using delicate silver chopsticks to eat some sort of cold dumplings stuffed with some sort of meat and vegetables, with some sort of sauce that tasted salty and sour and spicy at the same time, he tried to keep his mind on the appropriate litany of gratitude.

But he kept wondering if the gargoyle was really so far down from the windowsill as it seemed; and by natural extension, what would happen if he fell into the Abyss.

Perhaps he would fall for ever.

He thought about that long after the sprites bound to the tower had cleared away his tray. He did not bother to ask them their views. The sprites were, theoretically, rational creatures, but apart from their bounden duties they ignored him utterly.

If he did not fall for ever, he would either die, or survive and be expected to claim wherever he landed for the fiefdom of the Empire. His role, there in the tower, was to be an anchor for the Schooled magic; he had never learned any of the spells and ceremonies involved with conquering new lands.

He got up and looked out the the eastern window of this room, which was high above the bathing room floor. The Abyssal cloud roiled below him as mute and opaque as ever. It did not seem that there would be any land down there to claim. Merely the depths of the Shadow that had no name that he had heard of in any of the Nine Worlds.

★★★

The tower had one large room at the top that he used

as his main living space, with a small alcove off to one side with a sleeping couch. The shrine to the Emperor was located in the middle of the western wall, oriented to the far distance where the thin lines of magic converged at last in the Palace of Stars and the great golden throne of Astandalas.

There were windows to each of the eight directions, and shelves between them holding scrolls and books and miscellaneous tools of the wizard's trade. Apart from the eating couch and accompanying tables, there were some chests and numerous cushions, a few rugs, a standing harp, a wooden floor inscribed with a seven-pointed star, and a fireplace that had been burning a single log with a cheerful red-and-gold flame since he had arrived. There was a trapdoor in the centre of the ceiling, with a handle he had not worked out how to open, and on the northern edge of the room there was the stair leading down.

He was working his way through the books in the room. Most belonged to the tower's later inhabitants, wizards of one sort or another who had undertaken their studies in the peaceful solitude of the edge of the world, scholars devoted to their work and those devoted to the Empire.

Some of the books belonged to the tower's original builder, Harbut Zalarin whose mother had married the

Sun, but the young man had not realized that a certain old book he had found was one of them, and did not know that the old commonplace book was more dangerous than any of the grimoires or books of spells and cantrips.

He had found spells for levitation, but they were all of later vintage, and presupposed the full existence of Schooled magic. The tower was an anchor point for that intricate creation, but was not enmeshed in it, and the spells did not work. The young man did not know the reason for his continuing failures at Schooled magic, but had started nevertheless to follow the tracks of the older and more secret wild magic that were hidden in the references of the more acceptable books in the tower without quite knowing how far astray from prescribed paths he was going.

After ten minutes spent fruitlessly trying to work one of the levitation spells for the hundredth time, he went back to the bathing room and stared down at the gargoyle. The tower was made of alternating bands of rough dark and shimmering pale grey stone, much encrusted with moss and tiny ferns. The swallows built their nests below the window leagues and in a row under the gargoyles' necks. He watched for a while, but no other kind of bird landed on the stick nest.

He made himself go back up to his study to read the next chapter in his book on Voonran floral symbolism, which apparently was rather important if one wished to perform weather spells.

He couldn't concentrate on the niceties of distinction between types of carnations.

"I'm not supposed to go outside," he said aloud, rather startling himself. He went through periods of speaking out loud, but this had not been one of them. Yet today the network of ritual magic seemed almost to be listening, it was so strongly present in the room with him.

There was something gold and strange in the bird nest, and he had never been so curious in his life.

He walked restlessly around the tower. The sleeping chamber with the long divan and piles of soft cushions and silken blankets provided no rest. The windows faced west, to the setting—and here, alone he suspected of all places, the rising—Sun, so that first in the morning and last in the evening he could burn incense to the Emperor, descendant of the Sun through the line of Harbut Zalarin, glory of his people, fount of blessings, king of kings and mortal better worshipped than most gods.

The young man had been taught to pray, of course, with a hundred different invocations to the Emperor. He had not, however, come across the idea that one might pray outside of the set times and ceremonies.

It did not occur to him to ask assistance of the Emperor.

He went to the bathing room again. He peered cautiously out the window. The gold thing was still in the nest. The swallows were still flitting about, twittering gaily as they hunted insects.

He bent as far out the window as he dared. Down below—not in the Abyss but at the foot of the tower—possibly there was a tiny bit of land. He frowned near-sightedly at it, unable to judge the distance.

"There's no harm in seeing, is there?" he said to the swallows.

They ignored him as utterly as did the sprites.

★★★

The bathing room shared a floor with a privy and some sort of storage closet he had not examined closely. The fourth door was the one leading down. He opened it and peered down the narrow staircase as doubtfully as he had leaned out the window. His small motions echoed mournfully in the space down there, in a dank black hollow. He shuddered a little; and then he started down.

He kept his left hand on the wall. He had never been down the stairs before.

★★★

A few days before his sixteenth birthday his tutor had told him that his education was finished and that they would be parting ways, the tutor to retire to his family lands and himself to start his new life as a man grown to his estate and purpose in the Empire. Neither of them had been entirely sure what form his duty would take, but the young man had been curious about his new life and eager to experience the elaborate series of ceremonies that enacted his coming of age.

The ceremonies had surpassed his imagination, except that they had involved no great crowds or grand holocausts. The same four priest-magi who had performed all the previous great ceremonies had come and led him through the dances, the sacrifices, the bloodlettings and the bindings, the vesting and divesting and the hugely complex spells.

The young man had been delighted with the ceremonies, with the chance to observe such skilled wizards at work, and with the satisfying thought that at some fundamental level what he was and what he did mattered to the Empire of which he was so small a part.

Exhausted by the ceremonies, he had slept very deeply.

He had dreamed that he was being passed from hand to hand by a great chain of faceless and nameless people.

He had awoken to discover he was no longer in the house he had known all his life but rather in this stone tower at the farthest edge of the Empire, anchor for all its magic.

2

The wall was damp under his hand. He frowned nervously at the darkness and counted the steps as he went down. There were seventy-seven.

The room at the base of the tower was musty and strange smelling, as if the lair of long-gone beasts. (He had been reading, when the dry tomes of magic overwhelmed him, old poetry of adventures and heroism and bright deeds, which comprised a fair portion of the library upstairs.)

Making light was one of the first things he had learned, and so he warily illuminated the space around him. He let out a breath of mingled relief and disappointment that the cavernous space was utterly empty, without even a dragon scale or a coin to catch the light and feed his imagination.

The door to the tower was made of silvery grey logs bound with straps of woven copper gone green with time. The handle was a great iron ring set in the middle of the door, and it took him a goodly while to figure out that he had to turn it and then push the door open.

It was only after he stood blinking at the world outside that he realized it was the first door he had ever opened himself.

★★★

At ground level the dunes looked much bigger than they did from the windows above. White rocks led in a slanting line away from the door, between two steep slopes covered with the dull green grass, with little wild sea-clover blooming pink and white near the ground.

It was the usual hazy weather, mist boiling up from the Abyss, the Sun a pale disc in a white sky rived with startling blue. (Rived was his favourite new word; he had discovered it recently in a book of poems; he was pleased to find some use for it.)

The door was very heavy, or seemed so, hard to open, and even harder to keep open. He put his foot over the threshold to push it back all the way, and the wind caught it—or perhaps it was the action of one of the sprites—and slammed it back closed again with an enormous crash.

He fell over in surprise. Picked himself up, frowned, and turned the handle again. This time he could not push it open against the pressure, though he tried until his arms shook and his heart raced. At last he gave up, and slumped down against the door in some dejection, until a prickling uneasiness reminded him that it was time for the noon rituals and his lunch.

He was much slower about climbing up the stairs, and late to commence the small burnt offering. One pinch of snuff, one small white feather, three drops of blood, and a tiny waxy bead of fragrant ambergris. He rolled the ambergris around his fingers before dropping it into the miniature crucible. The magic of the Empire pulsed about him, tactile as a hand on his shoulder.

He felt very guilty for opening the door, and resolved to put the golden thing out of his mind.

He still couldn't concentrate on Voonran flower symbolism. He performed the first major tea ceremony, which was discretionary; choosing which of the four major or seven minor ceremonies for the day had always been one of his favourite things. But though he chose his favourite, dedicated to the spirits of fire, he did not feel either calmed or invigorated as he usually did; he felt anxious and unsettled.

He knew the names of the emotions from books. The feelings seemed to well up from somewhere usually inaccessible, through some door usually as firmly blocked as the tower's. The rituals, the ceremonies, the conventions and the routines, all were intended to prevent anxiety, worry, distress, fear. He was, he knew, granted a very great gift in that he knew with the uttermost certainty that his role in the Empire was to stay in his tower and perform his assigned rituals and keep the Empire safe from harm.

He could hardly abandon his sacred mission simply because he was curious about what a bird had found somewhere to place in its nest.

He put aside the book on flower symbolism and picked up a different book to take with him to sit by the fire.

It was one he had found slipped behind the Old Shaian epics, a small book bound in plain leather. It bore none of the gold or gems or even decorative tooling of the other books that had drawn his interest. He opened it now, to see that it was written in very old Shaian ideographs, with delicate calligraphy of exquisite mastery.

On the flyleaf was written, *The Commonplace Book of Harbut Zalarin.*

★★★

He grew absorbed in the account of an ancient wizard's day. Harbut Zalarin was from before the Empire; his grandson was Yr the Conqueror who had founded it. The thousands of years that various wizards had spent developing and elaborating the rituals of Schooled magic had not even begun in this book, and the way Harbut Zalarin spoke of magic was more like poetry than anything. The young man was entranced.

Harbut Zalarin noted things utterly foreign to his experience, and things of astonishing immediacy. The sensation of magic: the young man had never read anyone describe it so perfectly, or indeed at all. He felt he was reading his own thoughts at times, when Harbut Zalarin wrote of the magic he was doing or had done or had observed.

And then other times, he was thrown out of himself into wonder and confusion. Harbut Zalarin wrote about the weather at the time he awoke each day, with no explanation given. After a time the young man decided it must have been a component of his personal daily rituals, and therefore (as he had been taught to do) ceased his speculation. But he did wonder at the changing weather, and whether the ancient wizard was writing of this tower, which other books called the tower of Harbut Zalarin, and how much its circumstances had changed if he was.

In the months and years of his experience, it was always partly misty and partly sunny around the tower at the edge of the world. He always awoke at dawn for the first prayers, as he had done as far back as he could remember, and there was always the ebbing and flowing mist and the Sun running his courses.

His old life, in the big red house all by itself in the mountains, had incorporated occasional excursions out-of-doors, for his tutor studied wildflowers, and took him sometimes for walks. However, the red house was in the heartland of the Empire, and the weather there was perfect. Warm sunny days and mildly cool nights, rain falling only after dark; never snow, never storms, never hail. There had been one daytime windstorm, when he was twelve, and the wind had blown hard enough to bend the trees over.

That had been, he was told, because of the Emperor's displeasure with his request to learn swordsmanship and riding after reading too many old epics. Apart from the refusal to teach him (for there was no need for him to learn such barbaric arts), the library had been forbidden him and instead of epics he was forced to memorize the seven-volume *Manual of Etiquette*. He was destined for a life of seclusion and study; but he knew how to address every rank in the Empire, from lowest slave to the Emperor himself.

He had met, in his life, his parents, his tutor, the four priest-magi who performed the great ceremonies, and the seven servants of the red house.

He knew only the names of hail, snow, lightning, thunder.

He kept reading.

Sometimes Harbut Zalarin made little sketches or doodles on the page, in ink of several colours. Some framed pithy little aphorisms or things he wanted to remember, and the young man puzzled over these, perturbed at the nonchalance with which the ancient wizard wrote down his thoughts.

One stopped him:

What you name yourself you are.

He read this over several times before it occurred to him he didn't know what his own given name was.

He'd never been called by it. His tutor called him *savelin* or *chantling*, depending on whether what he'd been doing resulted in censure or endearment. *Savelin*, lordling; *chantling*, for the boy under enchantments.

The seven servants in the red house were very correct and proper about never addressing him directly, and probably did not know his name, either. His parents and the priest-magi presumably knew it, but as they only came to the red house once a year, for the annual seizin ceremonies, they had never needed to call him anything but boy.

Chantling, savelin, boy.

Harbut Zalarin was very concerned with names. There were lists of them elsewhere in the book, and a short passage discussing the nature of magic as akin to poetry, in that both were fundamentally the art of naming.

The young man put down the commonplace book and performed the mid-afternoon ritual perfunctorily, mind working in unaccustomed ways.

What you name yourself you are.

He kept going back to the page. Traced out the leaves of the plants in the frame around the words: ivy, columbine, strawberry. He'd seen them in his tutor's books of wildflowers, for they were not the plants of the red house or the tower.

What you name yourself you are.

It had never once occurred to him that he could name himself.

He got up to pace the tower room, back and forth from window to window, tracing out the seven-pointed star inscribed on the wooden floor in lines of silver and gold. He paused at one window, looking at the pale Moon sailing high above the mist in a deep blue sky. Turned after a blank stare at the silver line of the distant sea and the brilliant white spot of the Sun.

Stopped again at the eastern window to stare into the clouds of the Abyss. Two floors below him was the gargoyle sticking out, wreathed by swallows, with the stick nest visible like a hat between its ears.

He went back to the commonplace book, heart racing with feelings he could not name. Flipped through its pages, looking for he knew not what, some suggestion of action, some piece of advice, some rule to live by. Choosing which tea ceremony to perform or which book to read were the only decisions he had ever learned to make. He had not even ever tried to write his own poetry or invent his own spells.

He found no instructions. Many sentences and phrases and words that spoke to him in muffled voices, as incomprehensible as the winds calling around the tower, the sprites speaking to each other in voices like shadows, the birds singing or crying as they flew. Many intimations of doors he had not suspected existed. Many possibilities he could not even begin to imagine taking. Many blank pages that might have held secrets if only he'd had the key to opening them.

Naming himself was too enormous a first step. A lifetime of careful avoidance of names in favour of titles—Master Tutor, Sir and Madam, Magister and Magistra, Maid, Butler, Cook—could not be easily abandoned.

Savelin, Chantling, Boy: those were his names. His parents and the priest-magi had names and titles he had read in his *Manual of Etiquette*, but they remained as unreal to him as the Emperor to whom he prayed.

He went back to the bathing room. The swallows were spiralling around the gargoyle.

He put his hand on the windowsill, and then something he had read some time ago emerged into his mind, and he nearly ran upstairs to find the *Gesta Oloris*.

Olor was a hero of the early Empire. The young man had read the *Gesta* five or six times, never failing to be moved by the great arc of action, adventure, heroism, and final tragedy when Olor perished in a battle against the Tsorians. He found the scroll and unwound it quickly until he found the passage near the middle where Olor escaped from imprisonment in, yes, a tower.

> *And Olor of might and renown*
> *Took the clothes from his back and ripped them long*
> *And with the craft the Lady of Mists had taught him*
> *Wove them into one braid*
> *As long as the tower was high*

As long as his great endurance
Tied them to the bar in the window
And in the dark of the night made his escape.

The young man did not rip his clothing; he had been firmly punished for that as a boy, the first time he read the *Gesta*. He went to the storage room and picked through the strange items of clothing until he found a long strip of fabric, a foot wide and a dozen long, neatly folded in a basket.

It was scarlet as blood, and looked startling against the dark skin of his arms and the white of his simple tunic. Since he did not intend to escape the tower—where could he go?—he felt it long enough. He thought it most convenient it was already long and narrow, and since he had no idea how to make a plait (or indeed, quite what a plait was), he took it as it was into the bathing room.

There were no bars on the window; it wasn't a prison. After some consideration he discovered he could wrap one end of the fabric around the foot of the bath tub. It took him several attempts before it seemed at all secure when he tugged on it experimentally. But at last it seemed tightly enough wound—he knew nothing of knots—and then he was left with climbing out the window.

He draped the free end down first. The wind caught

it immediately, sending it flaming out over the abyss, a banner declaring allegiance to the little gods of fire or the Wind Lords of Kaphyrn or the first Lord of Ysthar or (if only it had had a yellow border) the third-ranked baron of Pfaschen on Alinor. He smiled to see it shining out so bravely against the clouds, even though clearly it would not hang quietly down as had the plait down which Olor had climbed.

He assumed this was because he had not plaited it, whatever that meant, but when he looked back at the scroll for assistance he saw that the next stanza described Olor undoing the end from around his waist.

He pulled the fabric back within and tied it around his waist, but when it was tight enough to stay up it was too short to reach the window, and when it was longer it was too loose and kept falling off. The young man sat on the edge of the tub and frowned out at the swallows swooping, the wild sprites laughing maniacally at only they knew what, and finally bethought himself to try tying it around his shoulder, like the formal mantle he had worn for one of the great ceremonies.

The window was waist high, too high for him to climb out of. He fetched a low stool out of the storage room, and, pleased with his ingenuity, clambered up.

Below him the swallows darted and swooped, the

gulls soared with unmoving wings, the half-invisible sprites rode their sky-horses, and the clouds moved incessantly. He thought of what might happen to the Empire if he fell and ceased performing his rituals.

He was not much given to imagining the future or the consequences of his actions; they had always been so circumscribed and carefully chosen, the answers had always been *do it right or else*. Neither had he anything beyond the vaguest sense of what the Empire actually was in terms of anything but magic and the lists of titles and addresses in the *Manual of Etiquette*.

He could name all the countries and provinces and domains of the Empire, who ruled them from which capitals, what their specialties were and when they had become part of Astandalas, what were their banners and their languages and their strict rank in the hierarchy of things.

He had seen the red house, its grounds, the encircling mountains, and the tower at the edge of the world.

Also, he did not think he would fall.

He was not nimble. He put one knee up on the ledge, and bounced awkwardly until he could get the other leg up beside it, and then he nearly pitched forward.

The fabric caught him before he could quite fall, and he nodded with satisfaction that Olor had guided him so well, and dismissed as a result any further concern for his safety. Olor had reached the ground safely; he was following Olor's example; surely there was nothing more to it.

He eventually managed to get one leg around, and then the other, and finally he was sitting on the window-sill with his legs dangling over. He swung them experimentally. There was a narrow ledge below him, out of which sprang the gargoyle's stone neck, and below that perhaps a small spit of land, and more certainly the Abyss.

He had a vague memory of Olor—or no, was it Daphnis of *Tikla Dor?*—wriggling out of another tower window to a tree—yes—that was Daphnis. She had turned, slid out on her belly, dropping down with her hands until her feet touched the branch.

Using the fabric to counterbalance him as best he could, he twisted around until he was resting on his armpits.

Unlike Daphnis, his feet did not touch.

It crossed his mind that had his tutor seen him, memorizing the *Manual of Etiquette* would have seemed a mild punishment. He could also feel the increasing constriction that indicated he was late for the next ritual. He almost tried to raise himself back up through the window, but for the fact he was nowhere strong enough to do so.

And so, without a prayer to any deity, he dropped.

He landed on the ledge with a wobble; the fabric kept him from tipping sideways. He leaned his forehead against the mossy stone of the tower and was amazed more at the feeling on his skin than at the fact that he was out-of-doors. He turned around.

The fabric was twisted around him such that he couldn't go more than a step away from the tower wall. When he tested its reach he stepped into a wind as buffeting and strong as that which had slammed the tower door in his face. He staggered back against the wall. The prickling in his head was growing. Upstairs he should have been lighting candles and chanting the forty-seventh of the psalms to the Emperor as Sun-in-Glory.

He shook his head and carefully extricated himself from the fabric. Daphnis had climbed down through the oak tree; he remembered the passage now. She'd come to a long narrow branch reaching out over the wall that enclosed her garden, and been unable to walk along its length. He'd never understood that difficulty, until he stood with his back pressed against the tower wall and looked at the eight feet he wanted to traverse.

A troupe of sprites galloped their sky-horses past him with wild yells and hooting laughter, and then it was just the swallows and the gulls and the clouds that went all the way down past the bottom of the world.

Daphnis had lain down on her stomach, legs on each side of the branch for balance, and used her feet to push herself along until she reached her destination.

He chanted the forty-seventh psalm as he followed suit. Without the candles the ritual was incomplete, but speaking the words helped. He felt the magic move about him, the enchantments grow quiescent by his words. He repeated the psalm three times, once for each of the candles upstairs, and with his face turned away from the wind, eyes watering from its pressure, he pushed himself forward until his hands reached the swelling stone carved with scales to represent the gargoyle's head.

He blinked away the tears and turned his head. There was a bird sitting in the nest.

A large black-blacked gull, it had a huge yellow beak and eyes that seemed to glitter malevolently at him. It was hunched down into the hollow of the nest, completely obscuring the golden thing.

With vague memories of the Cook batting her apron at him, he said, "Shoo."

The gull opened its beak, revealing a black tongue, and clacked it shut again.

"I need to reach under you," he said. The gull didn't do anything. He thought for a while, the wind whipping his clothes over his back. "If you would, I should be much obliged."

The gull sank its head into its shoulders and ignored him.

"I know you found it, but I can't think you need it, and I am very curious what it is."

The gull closed its eyes.

He reached forward with one cautious arm to slip his hand under the bird's body. For one astonishing moment he touched the soft warmth of its feathers and felt the fast beating heart.

★★★

He endured what felt an endless buffeting and many sharp pecks to his head, face buried in his arms to protect his eyes. When at last the affronted bird flew off he lay there for a while, gulping, shaking uncontrollably.

Finally the physical reaction passed, and he was able to move again. With one hand gripping the metal thing as tightly as he could, he pushed his way ever so slowly back to the wall of the tower. He hit stone with his rear and cried aloud with surprise at the touch before realizing what it was.

The scarlet cloth was flapping out in the wind again. He very slowly brought one leg up to the ledge, and then levered himself up against the tower wall until at last he was standing.

Something wet was trickling down his head and face. He thought it blood from the gull's attack, but when he wiped his face with the bottom of his tunic the streaks were greenish, not red. He frowned at it. He was used to blood and small cuts, integral components as they were of many of his rituals, but he had never sweated before except in illness. The green he thought a curious colour for a bodily fluid, but the poems never compared sweat to anything but the salt sea, and they often described the sea as green or blue. (He'd never smeared moss across himself, either.) He was pleased to discover the connection.

Even standing he could not reach the cloth. He transferred the golden thing to his left hand so he could reach up with his right, pressing his belly up against the stones of the tower. The wind snapped the red fabric to and fro, even more like a banner or a flag.

There were no sprites to ask or command assistance of, if they'd even listened to him—he wasn't sure they were even able to hear him. Instead he waited patiently until a gust or an unseen wild sprite snapped it down, whereupon he caught it, and very pleased indeed was he with this success. And then he stood there, mysterious golden object in one hand and loose end of the scarlet banner in the other, standing on a ledge with his back to the Abyss and his face to the tower at the edge of the world, and if perhaps he looked like Olor the Hero, he was rather less experienced in adventure.

The window was just at the level of his head. He could see the familiar room with sudden new perspective. The footed bathtub, enamelled in green and blue, with golden fixtures; the intricate mosaic tiles showing mythological sea scenes, the racks for towels and robes, the slatted floor under the dowser, and the various bathing utensils and ritual objects neatly in their places. The scarlet cloth wrapped around the tub was magnificently out of place, so magnificent he thought briefly of calling himself by its name.

"Scarlet," he said aloud, and knew immediately it was not the name for him.

Quickly, without thinking twice, he tossed his treasure into the bathing room. It landed in the tub; the enamel, or the metal, rang softly for some time afterwards.

He looked again at the cloth in his hands. Thought about the unfathomable drop below him, and the riddles to be answered and the name to be given awaiting him within.

He wrapped the cloth several times about his waist, pulling the end through and tucking it as tightly as he could, and then he grabbed the cloth with one hand and the far side of the sill with the other, and he jumped as high and hard as he could, in an action that in later years he always said was quite possibly the stupidest thing he had ever done—though that verdict was contested, if only by the initial blind drop out of the window.

Perhaps the gods of his ancestors or the Emperor of his prayers or the Sun and Moon whose near relation had built the tower were looking out for him, for the loose twists did not come undone until after he had wriggled and twitched his ungainly way back into the bathing room. He bumped his chin on the edge of the tub and spent a good quarter of an hour disentangling himself from the scarlet cloth, and there was blood on the floor when he at last he stood, triumphant, to collect his treasure out of the tub.

He took the scarlet cloth upstairs with him as a kind of trophy of his adventure.

3

The golden thing was a piece of worked metal, about as long as his hand. The main part of it was a rod, narrower than his finger, like an eating stick or a pen barrel. One end was flattened and worked with wire and metal beads of gold and silver into the shape of the Sun embracing the Moon one on side, and the Moon embracing the Sun on the other. A pattern of tiny stones glittered along the barrel, and at the other end the gold was worked into a strange geometry of grooves and protuberances.

The young man had never seen a key, and had formed from his books the mental image of a sort of stone that worked sympathetic magic on locks to open doors whenever he read the word. He turned the golden key over and over in his hands and wondered what magic it was intended to perform.

Since he had no other resources, he turned to his books to give him guidance. What he found, however, further along from the unsettling comments about names in the commonplace book, was a spell to reveal or remove enchantments—the ideograph could have meant either—by translating the enchantment to another receptacle.

He frowned over this as he performed the sunset rituals, with extra diligence after his disobedience.

The object probably belonged to Harbut Zalarin, son of the Sun and nephew of the Moon, and very likely it was enchanted.

He bathed and returned to sit by the fire in his robe, looking at the table on which he had placed the book and the key.

Harbut Zalarin's spell did not seem very complicated, or not to someone had spent many months puzzling through the hints of wild magic in the texts left by discreet wizards of Astandalas, reticent to speak of forbidden magic even in books intended to stay in the tower at the farthermost edge of the Empire. Harbut Zalarin's spell involved none of the tools or materials or rituals of Schooled magic: just the words, the will, and the focused talent.

Among the items left by the Schooled wizards was a necklace made of black and white crystals set in gold, probably meant for a gift-offering left uncompleted. The young man set the necklace on the table before him, laid the key beside it, and after gathering his thoughts and arranging himself into a meditative posture, he spoke the spell.

He was not expecting the result to be quite so spectacular as it was.

While he sat on the mat before the table, mouth agape, the magic in the tower began to coruscate, to pulse, to shimmer, and to move. It gathered itself out of corners, plucked at the folds of his clothing, swirled over his skin like the waters of the bath he had just left. It was visible to his ordinary vision, a gathering explosion of golden sparks, filling the air with power and making it hard to breathe.

He sat very still, heart pounding with excitement, as the magic poured upwards around him. He had thought the wind outside the tower door strong: this was far stronger, buffeting him from all directions, slamming at his body and his mind. He had grasped the golden key, however, out of determined curiosity, and determined curiosity kept him focused on his goal, the translation of the enchantment to the necklace so he could see what it was and learn.

His attention narrowed under the pressure of magic until the ring of black and crystal filled his mind. The golden magic belled outwards, trying to tug him away from his intention, but with an effort far surpassing anything he had ever done before he held to that purpose.

How long he sat there unmoving under the grip of the magic he didn't know. Finally the magic gathered into a restless unity under him. He shook in awe and trepidation and fear as he spoke the final three words of the spell, the binding of the outer enchantment to its new home.

With an awful boom the magic coalesced into the necklace; and he fainted.

4

He awoke again to himself in the dark.

There were three sources of light: the eternally burning log in the fireplace, starlight from the eight windows, and a flickering, pulsating glow from the necklace on the table.

He sat up, feeling dizzy. Put a hand out to steady himself, and was surprised to see how it shook. He sat there assessing his physical sensations with some wonder at their newness and raw strength: he was dizzy, shaking, somehow soft inside himself, his throat tight and his mind feeling bruised. He wiped his face with his hands.

"Not so simple as it seemed, was it?" he said to himself. It was something his tutor had often said to him, when he blithely launched into something new.

The young man smiled, remembering with abrupt clarity one of those occasions, when he had tried to climb a bookshelf in the library to reach some bright-jacketed book from a high shelf, and pulled all the books down upon him when he fell. How much trouble he'd been in for that mischief—and then the book turned out to be a grammar of Renvoonran, which his tutor had decided he should learn as his punishment.

That was definitely the most difficult piece of magic he had ever performed. He wiped his face again, sat up straighter, and stared at the table. The stones of the necklace were no longer transparent black and clear crystals, but rather smokey and opaque, magic-haunted, each stone the terminus of one or three or a dozen spells that stretched around the tower and far off into the west.

He looked at the key, which looked exactly the same as it had earlier, and he looked around the room, which also looked and felt as it had all the time he'd lived there, and then he was abruptly too weary to begin guessing what else he might inadvertently have disenchanted, and therefore tottered off to bed.

It was only when he awoke a second time, far after dawn, that he realized it was himself.

★★★

He knelt before the window to perform the first ritual of the day, and discovered halfway through the invocation that something was deeply amiss.

He stumbled over his words and nearly dropped the incense, and finally he rocked back on his heels and stared out the window at the Sun well away on his journey.

Eventually he realized what it was: the ritual was empty. He'd said the right words and performed all the correct actions, and, with his heart racing with panic that he was so late, and guilt for all his errantry and mischief the day before, all that with much more focused intent and diligence than usual, almost as much as he'd used for the disenchantment—and—nothing.

It was like plucking a harp string and making no sound at all.

He stumbled through the rest of his rituals, the bath and the anointings and the chanting and the incense and the prayers, and all the while he felt as if his feet were drifting out from under him.

In the tower room two trays sat waiting beside the necklace. One held the gold goblet of water and gold platter of buns that was the first meal, the other an elaborate pyramid of colour-coordinated fruit that was the second.

He lay down on the eating couch, reached out automatically for food—and hesitated over which plate to take from.

He got up in immediate disquiet, paced around a few times. South window, north, southwest, northeast, west, east. His eye was avoiding the necklace and the key; landed on the book.

What you name yourself you are.

Savelin, Chantling, Boy were the names he had been given, and not known better than to accept. Northeast, southwest, north, south. Something was building within him: hunger or fear or some magic, he couldn't tell.

At last he went to the necklace. The intricate spells anchored in it had been no dream of the night. They hummed in their places, the most powerfully enchanted object he had ever seen, even more than the things the priest-magi had brought for the great ceremonies of binding.

When they bound him, he thought slowly.

He reached out a cautious finger to one slender, small spell, but before he could touch it recoiled so strongly he found himself unwitting on the far side of the room.

He sat in the window embrasure, sucking at his finger and staring wide-eyed at the necklace. It had shocked him: physically as shuffling feet on a carpet might, psychically as had the spellcasting of the night before—and emotionally as nothing ever had, for he knew the inner nature of the spell he had brushed against from the outside.

Accept what you are told.

When he was able to bear looking at it again, he followed that slender, small spell as it moved from the stone nearest the clasp of the necklace and wound its way between all the other spells before finally anchoring itself back in itself. The root of all his life: the undemanding acceptance of everything that happened to him.

These were *his* enchantments.

★★★

He regarded the necklace with a mixture of fascination, wariness, and another emotion for which he did not, initially, have a name.

It began as akin of hollow feeling in his belly, and then as it started to grow it became more like a flame burning there, like a small bright sun of astonishing purity and uncomfortable strength.

He watched the necklace, or rather the streamers of magical light emanating from it, for a long time. The rectangles of sunlight on the floor stretched and shifted their angle as the Sun ran his course. The magic moved, too, spells crossing from one stone to another, the light changing in a pattern whose timing he knew intimately.

When it came time for the noon rituals he stirred in the window embrasure, about to begin them, the habitual action nearly as strong as the enchantment—when that unfamiliar fiery emotion rose up in his throat and made him say, "No."

He shivered at the sound of his voice. There was an edge to it he'd never heard from himself, a sharpness to the tone that matched some inward sharpness that was slowly being revealed as the uprooted remnants of his enchantments continued to fall away.

The enchantments wove an elaborate structure around the necklace, hundreds of them of such complexity he knew he could sit there learning the ways of Schooled magic for the rest of his life, and probably come to be one of the great magi himself.

He said, "No," again, uttering the word as firmly as if he were claiming unknown lands for the Emperor. The rejection was immediate and irrevocable, and came from the place of fire within himself.

The sprites brought the tray containing the ritual's implements and his lunch, and set it beside the necklace. He was hungry, but he stayed in the window embrasure to see what would happen. No point, he thought, in doing empty rituals. It was a strange thought.

The magic in the necklace moved: spells lit up in sequence, wove between each other, under over, through, so the air thrummed like a plucked harp string, and the ritual implements pinged lightly as the magic touched them.

After the magic had resettled he went to the table and took the plate of food before retreating again to his spot at the window. The meal was yellow rice and bright red sauce over chicken and vegetables, with flaked almonds and green herbs decorating the top. Flat bread served as both utensil and antidote to the spiciness of the stew. He ate with gusto, and as he used the bread to mop up the last of the sauce he wondered, not for the first time, both where it had come from and how it had arrived piping-hot and delicious in the tower at the edge of the world.

For the first time he wondered what it might be like to go find out.

The mere thought made his hands shake. He dropped a piece of bread and stared at the smear it made across the floor. Go find out?

He looked at the enchantments. One of them had always prevented that second question from crossing his mind.

Go find out.

After lunch there were candles to light and invocations to say. Before thinking he started to say the words for the lighting spell; and then he stopped, and after hesitating a few moments, watching the candles sitting unlit on the table next to the glittering necklace as the magic moved without him. Awkward, unsure, uncomfortable with himself, he picked up the *Commonplace Book of Harbut Zalarin* and the scarlet cloth and walked all the way down the stairs to the bottom door of the tower without stopping.

He took a deep breath, turned the handle, and pushed open the door. It opened easily.

He took another deep breath and stepped outside.

★★★

A bank of fog surrounded the tower. Going down the stairs he'd half-formed the plan to sit outside and read, but after he went two or three feet away from the door he stopped, bewildered and increasingly chilled by the swirling mist. After a few minutes spent staring at the blankness he retreated back inside.

The climb up the seventy-seven stairs seemed very long. When he reached the bathing-room floor he stopped for breath. He was sweating again, and washed his face. As he dried himself off he looked out the window at the gargoyle and the empty stick nest. The angry gull had not returned.

After sitting on the stool he'd left under the window for a while, it occurred to him that it might be fun to see what else there was in the storage room. Accordingly he went next door, and proceeded to spend a very happy few hours opening boxes and trunks and wardrobes and trying to figure out what all these intriguing items were.

Hunger at last drove him up to the tower room for supper. It no longer felt so welcoming a space, not with the magic buzzing around the necklace. He felt too un-settled after eating to read Harbut Zalarin after all, so he pulled down his favourite poems and read about Daphnis and Olor and Tzu-tzên and Aurelius Magnus until it was far too late in the night.

Every time he came to a new character he tried out their name, speaking it aloud to hear its sound on the air, but none of them seemed quite to answer. He no-ticed some names trailed meanings after them, and others named the one person and nothing more. He thought perhaps he'd rather have a name all to himself, one he could—like Olor or Hu Liang—make famous by his own doings ... but still, nothing came.

As he read the end of the *Gesta Oloris* he discovered the name for the hot fire in his breast. When Olor realized his betrayal by his blood brother, the poet said, "his breast lit with fire/ with the white flame of righteous anger/ and burning like the Sons of Thunder" (a gloss explained that these were the gods of war), "Olor lifted up his sword,/ fine-cleaving Ordnamur,/ ready at last to die."

The young man read the words over and over again, the thrill the lines had always given him blending with the fire in his own breast as he realized that what he felt— what caused him this fiery pain, this strange sense almost of exaltation—was anger. Righteous indignation—now he connected them other words rushed to mind. Fury. Rage. Wrath.

He did not sleep well that night. He woke before dawn the next morning, determined that he would not fail the heroes of his beloved poems, neither Daphnis nor Olor nor Tzu-tzên nor any of the others. He would not stay in the tower, enchanted into obedience, nor disenchanted and afraid.

No. He would go off and find out where the spiced stew came from, go see the countries whose names and rulers and heraldry and imports and exports he had learned by rote, and—this was where the books were particularly clear—he would avenge himself and die in a blaze of glory and justice.

He decided this at sunrise, and by sunset had despaired of ever leaving, for he was not quite so naive as to set off blindly into the fog with no supplies at all. The poems were fairly clear on the necessity of supplies.

He went to the storage room and examined all the piles he'd made earlier. There was one old leather bag in the back corner of the storage room, perhaps a foot long and as much around, with a strap to go over his shoulder and handles to carry it by the rest of the time.

He put the *Commonplace Book of Harbut Zalarin* and the scrolls containing the *Gesta Oloris*, *The Seven Classical Poets*, and a few texts of magic in it, followed by the red cloth and a piece of blue fabric with yellow swirls on it he found rather appealing. He was going to add some paper and bottles of ink, but the bag was too full.

He carried the bag upstairs and unpacked it again. Clearly he needed it to carry more than it did on its own merits. He frowned at it, nibbled his lip, paced back and forth, and spent the better part of the next month figuring out how to enchant it to hold whatever he put in it.

Every half hour or hour he would emerge out of his scribbles and attempts to concoct the spell with a name on the tip of his tongue: Aurora, Fin-hêlad, Brazenose the

Pure.

These were not his names. Tenebra, Peter, the Kor, Wellamotte, Zurifne. He wrote them down in the margins of an empty notebook he'd found, lists of names for the first beginnings of his own commonplace book. At one point while he was pondering his list, a line jumped into his mind with such force he jumped physically:

In the Land of Blue Meadows, Tenebra waited for the grockles to come.

After he calmed his suddenly-racing heart, he wrote down the words and stared at them. Tenebra? The Land of Blue Meadows? Grockles?

He thoughtfully wrote *grackles?* above *grockles*, and was quite certain the line was not about blackbirds of any sort. He had the image of a young woman standing in the middle of a field of blue flowers, dressed in a cloak as scarlet as the banner he'd draped across the shrine to the Emperor to hide it, waiting for something to come.

He considered this mental picture for a long time before he realized it was the beginning of a poem. One of his very own.

He wrote, *Tenebra*, above the poem, and then, after a while spent staring at the list of names again, crossed it out and wrote *Aurora*, and then because the words just arrived in his mind from somewhere, added, *and the Pea-*

cock, and then, his pen suddenly scritching freely across the book, spattering ink in his excitement, he wrote: *by the revolutionary poet Fitzroy the Adventurer.*

He nibbled at the end of his pen for a bit, something not sounding quite right about this last—perhaps Adventurer wasn't right—but Fitzroy, yes, Fitzroy was it. He rolled the sound of it in his mind and on his tongue, speaking it aloud in as many tones he could contrive. Fitzroy. Fitzroy. *Fitzroy*. Fitzroy.

Yes.

He then packed:

A pile of useful books, magic and poetry, and a few others that seemed simply curious that he wanted to read.

Twelve silk slippers in twelve different colours, because he thought them pretty; though as his feet were quite large, and the slippers had been made for young princesses, none of them fit. He did not let this bother him. The poems might be clear on the need to take supplies, but they left it up to his imagination what those supplies should consist of, and the young man felt that the slippers would come in handy at some point or other in the mysterious future opening before him.

Seven lengths of cloth, nearly all the clothes in the tower, a few blankets, one cushion. He found the hatch and attempted to communicate his desires to the enchanted pantry. Fortunately it was more perceptive of his need than he himself was, and provided him with the imperishables of many lands. Almost none of these, whether the jerky or the dried fruit or the amphorae of oil and preserved fish or the beautifully carved spice cabinet, were known to him, but after a lifetime spent eating whatever he was given, he assumed he would have no difficulties with any of it.

Three pairs of sandals that did fit him. Paper and pens and ink, the small harp that he could fit within—the great standing harp in the corner of the tower was, alas, chained to its place, and he could not work out how to undo it.

The ancient Shaian literature he loved rarely spoke of money except in the form of gold, so he scoured the tower for items made of that metal. Apart from his prize from the gargoyle, he found several rings, necklaces, and a small box of ingots. He paused, putting the box into his bag, wondering what people used the gold for if not to make jewellery.

And then at last, one grey and misty mid afternoon, he set off into the fog with one parting glance at the tower when he shut the door with deliberate care behind him.

He spoke to the sprites, who continued to ignore

him, and the swallows and the gulls and the stones of the tower and all those intricate enchantments anchored in the necklace:

"I am Fitzroy. The poet. And adventurer."

He had had enough of magic, he'd decided. He waited a moment, but, naturally, nothing happened. He shrugged phlegmatically and then laughed aloud when he realized that *nothing had happened*, and he was free.

Smiling broadly, he shouldered his bag and set off for the peopled lands.

The Tower at the Edge of the World is the first of the infamous Fitzroy Angursell of the Red Company's many adventures. (How he comes up with his surname and the Red Company is founded is matter of the first novel of the Red Company's doings, *Small Rebellions*, which is forthcoming.) You may be interested in *The Bride of the Blue Wind*, the first story of the Sisters Avramapul, whose lives will intertwine with Fitzroy's, and in *Victi Magnificamur*, which treats of the legacy of the Red Company many decades in the future.

You are also welcome to visit my author website and join my mailing list for information about new releases, both available at www.victoriagoddard.ca.

Novels also available from Underhill Books:

Stargazy Pie (Greenwing & Dart Book 1)

A dozen or so years after the Fall of Astandalas, magic is out of fashion, but good manners never are.

Jemis Greenwing returned from university with a broken heart, a bad cold, and no prospects beyond a problematic inheritance and a job at the local bookstore.

Ragnor Bella is a placid little market town on the road to nowhere, where Jemis' family affairs have always been the main source of gossip. He is determined to keep his head down under the cover of his new employer's devastating mastery of social etiquette, but falls quickly under the temptation of resuming the friendship of Mr. Dart of Dartington—land agent to his older brother the squire and beloved local daredevil—who is delighted to have Jemis' company for what is, he assures him, a very small adventure.

Jemis expected the cut direct. The secret societies, criminal gangs, and illegal cult to the old gods come as a complete surprise.

Till Human Voices Wake Us

Raphael is a secret mage, responsible for the world's magic, whose efforts to prevent the end of the world are impeded rather more by the unexpected arrival of his long-lost brother—and the well-meaning interference of his friends—than by his enemy.

Raphael is not afraid of magic, but love is a different matter.

A retelling of the myth of Orpheus set in a mostly-real modern-day London.

Other short stories currently available are "Scheherezade" (about what happens to eponymous storyteller on the last of the thousand and one nights), "Inkebarrow," (in which William Shakespeare, taking a wrong turning beyond the fields he knows, encounters the Black Bull of Inkebarrow), and "Rook," in which the Prince of the Fairies learns a lesson.